T0247750

SANDI VAN

An imprint of Enslow Publishing

WEST **44** BOOKS™

**Please visit our website, www.west44books.com.
For a free color catalog of all our high-quality books,
call toll free 1-800-398-2504.**

Cataloging-in-Publication Data

Names: Van, Sandi.
Title: Caught in the haze / Sandi Van.
Description: New York : West 44, 2022. |
Series: West 44 YA verse
Identifiers: ISBN 9781978595989 (pbk.) |
ISBN 9781978595972 (library bound) |
ISBN 9781978595996 (ebook)
Subjects: LCSH: Children's poetry, American. |
Children's poetry, English. | English poetry.
Classification: LCC PS586.3 V36 2022 |
DDC 811'.60809282--dc23

First Edition

Published in 2022 by
Enslow Publishing LLC
29 East 21st Street
New York, NY 10011

Copyright © 2022 Enslow Publishing LLC

Editor: Caitie McAneney
Designer: Tanya Dellaccio

CPSIA compliance information: Batch #CW22W44: For further information contact
Enslow Publishing LLC, New York, New York at 1-800-398-2504.

This book is dedicated to my son Paul, whose speed and energy on the field always leave an impression.

THE FINAL MINUTE

Final game of the season.

The score: 1–0.

How much time, ref?
I ask.

> *Less than a minute,*
> he says,
> glancing at his watch.

Coach paces
the sidelines.

Parents scream
from their seats.

Less than a minute.

We can do this.
We can hold them.

I can do this.
I can hold them.

Him.
I can hold HIM.

The fastest kid
in the league.
No. No way.

I'M the fastest kid
in the league.

Here he comes,
on a perfect pass
from the center mid.

Here he comes.
I'm ready.

We face off.

Contain, contain,
eyes on the ball,
not the feet.

He passes back to center

     and takes off down the line.

         Hands clap for a return pass.

I don't have to look.
I know there's only
one man back there.

Our center D,
our sweeper,
and he's not fast enough.

It's up to me.

I turn on my heel
ready for the chase.

Dig,
dig,
dig.

You got this, Tae.

Dig,
dig,
dig.

The forward receives
the pass at his feet.

Looks up—
eyes the net—
sees the perfect shot
to tie the game
and send us into OT.

But
 what he
  doesn't see
   is me
    right
     behind
      him,
       closer,
        closer,
         on
          his heels.

I hear Dad's voice
in my head:

Keep it clean, Tae.
Keep it clean.

I lean in with my shoulder
just enough to throw him
off balance.

Reach my foot out,
push the ball away.

He stumbles
but doesn't trip.

Ball—
I got ball—
no whistle.

The forward whips around.

In shock?
Anger?

And then the whistle comes
high and fast,
three tweets,
short—short—long.

GAME OVER.

1-0

Game over—we won.

WE WON!

The sweeper chants,
DEFENSE! DEFENSE! DEFENSE!

He tackles me from the side.
Nice run, man.
You saved our skins.

I smile.
High-five.

Line up for handshakes
and *great games.*

I feel
like I can
conquer
anything.

END OF AN ERA

We celebrate
with ice cream
at the local stand
two blocks from the soccer fields.

Me, Mom, Dad,
and my little brother Aaron.

The team's there, too.

And Coach.

Nice game, Tae!
they all shout.

More high fives,
handshakes.

Coach slaps me on the back.

Varsity for sure, he says.
See you at tryouts?

I smile
but shake my head.
Lower my eyes and
stare at my chocolate-vanilla twist.

What?
You've got the chops for it.
This kid here, he—

Mom interrupts
with a grin that looks forced.

We're moving this summer, she says.
Tae will be at Westgate in the fall.

Coach smiles back.

But I notice
for a brief moment,
the smile fades slightly.

He knows about Westgate.
He knows, and I know.

Westgate, eh?

A pause, and then:

They're lucky to have ya.
And with your speed,
varsity for sure.

His words repeat,
but they sound different.

Sharper.
With an edge of doubt.

Coach looks at me, Mom, Dad,
and back to me.

Good luck to ya, kiddo.

Yeah.
Good luck.

BETTER FOR WHO?

It isn't like
anyone asked me
what I
wanted.

Nope.

Mom brought in
a stack
of cardboard boxes
and
dropped
them
on my bed.

Good news, she said.
*They accepted our offer
on the new house!*

*Better neighborhood,
better schools.*

We move in about a month.

Start packing.

CHANGE

When Mom announced
that we were moving,
my heart sank.

I hate change.

Not Aaron.

He WOO-HOOed
and threw
his stuffed dinosaur
at me.

*No more sharing a room
with you, Boogerhead,*
he shouted
in the annoying voice
he saves for me.

I try to focus on
the positive.

A room of my own.

No more hiding under the covers,
earbuds in,
watching the latest episode
of *Attack on Titan*.
No more endless stories
about *Monsters from the Great Beyond*—

Aaron's made-up universe.
Greek myths
meet modern-day zombies.

I think about his stories
as I pack the last of my things
into a box.

And wonder if he'll still tell them
through the wall between our new rooms.

HOUSE SHAPED

We
pull up to our
new house with its too-
short driveway and perfect green
grass. It looks like every
other house on the street.
As if someone took a 3D
house-shaped stamp and
stamped them all out one

after the other.

And forgot

to leave enough

space between

them for a backyard.

NEW IN TOWN

Not that I imagine
anyone plays
OUTSIDE
around here.

Considering
it's a warm summer day
and the only noise
is music coming from Aaron's earbuds.

The chirpy sound
of some cartoon theme song.

Dude.

I poke my brother
in the leg.

DUDE.

    Heh?

We're here.

Aaron looks out the window.
His reaction the exact opposite of
my stomach-twisted
sickness.

    Sweet.

ONE OF THESE THINGS IS NOT LIKE THE OTHER

It doesn't take long to realize
Aaron and I
don't match
our new neighborhood.

I watch through
my new bedroom window
as people pass by.

Dog walkers.
Couples hand in hand.
Babies in strollers.

All white.

I wonder if my parents
thought about that
when they bought the house.

Thought about how we'd stick out
like Korean sore thumbs.

It never seems to bother Aaron.
He fits in everywhere he goes.
Makes friends faster
than I can run down the field.

NOT ME

I prefer the comfort
of my online friends.

The ones who
understand.

Who don't expect me
to fit their molds
and expectations.

Trouble is,
they can't help me
on the first day of school
or out on the field.

Making the team
(at least around here)
means I need to find a way
to fit in.

FIRST THINGS FIRST

To achieve the goal
requires strength, speed, endurance.
It won't come easy.

MIDNIGHT

might not seem
like the ideal time
for a workout.

But it is.

For me, anyway.

I tiptoe out of
my fancy new room.
Down the
fancy new stairs.
And out the
fancy new front door.

Make my way
into the night.

The air thick and quiet,
the streets darker here
than at our old place.

I warm up with a stretch.
Cue the beats in my ears.
Run.

Stop every mile
for a round of push-ups,
hands firm against
the raw pavement.
Sprints measured by
the rows of houses.
Harder here because I haven't yet
learned their distance.

I push my body
until my lungs burn
and sweat dribbles
down my back.

KING OF EVERYTHING

Mom takes me for a tour
of my new school.

We're greeted at the front door
by a tall kid with blond hair
tucked under a baseball hat.

Name's Shane, he says,
extending his hand.
Nice to meet you.

I'm head of the orientation committee,
senior class president,
captain of the soccer team.

He stares at Mom as if
his string of titles
means she can trust him.

His too-wide grin
says something else.

She smiles and nods her head,
puts her hand on my shoulder.

I try not to cringe.

Wonderful, she says.

*Tae here is an
excellent soccer player.*

*Maybe you can tell him
more about the team?*

Shane laughs
this strange
throat laugh.

Yeah, sure, of course.

I want
to crawl
inside
my hoodie
and die.

WESTGATE HIGH

This school is
way too big
and way too clean
and way too much
for me to handle.

TEXT MESSAGE

Captain's practice Mon.
See u there?
Shane

SUNDAY NIGHT

Mom is over the moon
about my new school
and its *amazing opportunities*.

Her words,
not mine.

The night before
my first practice,
she serves spaghetti and meatballs.
Tells me to *carbo-load*
and *go get 'em!*

I try not to roll my eyes,
but I can't stop the heavy sigh
from escaping my lips.

Oh, Tae, she says.

*You know
we love you.*

No matter what happens.

You love me.
Sure.

But if I don't make the team,
will I love myself?

DETHRONED

I go from being
number one
the star
king of the mountain

to just another
sweaty underclassman
lined up with all the other
sweaty underclassmen

waiting
for
our
execution.

GREATNESS

I pull my long hair into a ponytail
at the base of my neck.

Yank up my socks.

Breathe deeply.

The sides of my stomach
are sore from last night's
round of sit-ups.

Shane towers over us
like a Greek god from
one of Aaron's stories.

All right, noobs,
listen up.

This isn't the soccer field
behind the playground.

This is the big leagues.

Two weeks to tryouts—
and you, my friends,
have a backstage pass
to greatness.

MESSAGE FROM THE KING

Shane holds up two fingers,
first facing out,
then pointing at
each of us in turn,

his eyes like flames.

If you think
any of it will
be easy—
quit now.

Walk away.

He waves at us
with his hand.

Waits.

No one moves.

MOTLEY CREW

We run
      and run
            and run.

Midmorning sun
turns to melting
afternoon heat.

Then—
one thousand touches on the ball
before our first water break.

I drink like a man
lost in the desert.

Shane claps his hands before
we even have a chance to
catch our breath.

Let's go—
time for drills.

Other boys arrive.

Toss their bags
onto the grass.

They slap hands
and pat each other's backs.

Pat, pat.

Lift their heads
toward us—the noobs—
red-faced and
covered in sweat.

Half-smiles for the boys
they recognize.

Not for me.

Not for the new kid.

They stare a beat too long
at my hair
(too thick, too black, too long)
my skin
(too dark)
the shape of my eyes.

Until I see the face of someone
I recognize:

Luke.

FRIENDS FOR LIFE

Luke and I met
a million summers ago.

I was five
and he was seven.

The age when everyone is a friend
as long as you have something—
anything—in common.

Our common ground?

Bugs.

We played in a mound of dirt
behind picnic benches
while our mothers discussed
the challenges of adoption.

Swapped stories about
wait times
and home studies
and *can you believe the paperwork?*

There were other kids there,
mostly girls.

We ignored them.

Our focus locked on a trail
of ants carrying crumbs
twice their size.

Look at that,
I remember my mother saying.

Tae and Luke really hit it off.

Bet they'll be friends for life.

SPOILER ALERT

We weren't.

FRIENDS FOR A SEASON

Don't get me wrong.

Our friendship was fun
while it lasted.

Until going
to adoption group meetings
became just another calendar item
on our family's busy schedule.

Until one day, when we did go,
Luke wanted to flirt with girls
instead of look for bugs.

He's an early bloomer,
I heard my mom say.

To me, on the car ride home,
Maybe you're better off without him.

THE PARTY

I remember the last time
we saw each other.

A Chinese New Year party
in sixth grade.

Luke sat in the corner
and complained.

From his angry mouth
the words *freaks* and *losers*
and *why do we have to celebrate this
stupid holiday?*

It's not like I'm Chinese.

Our eyes met.

Like it was somehow my fault
he had to be there.

Like he had forgotten our
friendship ever existed.

        Hey, I managed to say.

Hopeful he'd remember.

No offense, man,
he mumbled.
This whole thing is stupid, right?

I wanted to agree,
wanted to take the side
of this person I thought was
my "friend for life."

But I liked the parties.

I liked the food,
the costumes,
the chance to stomp on
a giant row of bubble wrap.

So, I shrugged my shoulders
and said,
        I'm not Chinese either.

I'M NOT CHINESE EITHER

That was the last thing
I said to Luke.

And now
he's standing
over me
blocking
the sun—
a flicker
of recognition
in his eyes.

Hey, man,
you trying out for the team?

SAVED?

I've heard the rumors.
I know about what goes down
at Westgate.

If you want to be part of the team,
you need to be willing
to do whatever it takes.

Right now
whatever it takes
is mending a bridge
I'd rather set on fire.

LUKE

GOOD INFLUENCE

I recognized his face
right away.

Who could forget
the Asian kid
Mom hoped would
become my best friend?

*Tae seems like such
a good influence,* she'd said.

Yeah, well I sure hope
he doesn't
bring his goody two shoes
onto the field.

You wanna run with this crowd—
you need to break some rules.
Hey man, I say.

You trying out for the team?

He nods.

There's a look of
fear in his eyes.

Does he think I'm gonna punish him?

Or save him from getting punished?

THE SPEECH

Other than our
oh-so-friendly
hello,
Luke avoids me
for the rest of practice.

He falls in
with the other
upperclassmen.

They bark at us like
a training scene
in a war movie.

I wait for someone to say
something about
separating the men from the boys
or some other corny phrase.

Nope.

Shane steps forward.

Shushes the other guys.

Says,
The next two weeks
of your lives will be
nothing short of hell.

The challenges
in front of you
are meant to
make you stronger.

We will come out
on the other side
united.

SHANE = FUTURE PRESIDENT OR CULT LEADER?

Not gonna lie—
the guy has charm.

In a part-inspiration,
part-terror
kind of way.

NEVER-ENDING PRACTICE

After Shane's speech:
more sprints
more touches
more drills.

Breaks for
the returning team members,
but not for us noobs.

You drink when we say you drink!

A kid I don't know
turns to me,
red in the face.

>He says—out of breath
>but full of sarcasm—
>*You hurl when we say you hurl.*

I laugh,
then wince.

The sides of my stomach
scream in pain.

AFTER PRACTICE

I text Mom,
hoping she'll have pity
and pick me up.

Someone taps me
on my shoulder
as I hit send.

Hey, man.

> *Luke.*
> *Hey.*
> *Nice to*
> *see you again.*

Yeah, you too.

What'd ya think?

Pretty intense, yeah?

I nod.

Intense.

That's one word for it.

LUKE

MISTAKE

Mom wants to know
how practice went.

She wants to know,
*Was that Tae? The boy from
our adoption group?*

Mom wants to know
if I was nice to him.

> *Obviously,* I say.

Like she expects me to admit
to being a jerk.

Wait, was I?

No.

I was nice to him.

NO PAIN, NO GAIN

The next day
is more of the same.

Long laps
around the field
a million times
followed by
lung-crushing sprints.

Foundations, touches,
toe taps, keep-away—
who's got the killer moves?

Two-minute planks—
the sweat dripping
into my eyes.

I tell myself it's not that bad.

It's
not
that
bad.

I GOT YOUR BACK

And then
I see the
seniors
stand up
and press
the soles
of their
spikes
into the
backs
of the
boys
whose
backs
aren't
straight.

Screams of pain
escape their lips.

They are told to
be *QUIET!*

I wait for my turn.

No.

The name he calls out
hits my core.

He pulls at the edges of his eyes
to make his point.

The other players laugh.

I can control my hair
and the zits on my face.

(Maybe. Mom says I need
to eat better and wash
with special soap.)

But I can't control
being Asian.

I open my mouth to protest.

To tell him it's not okay
to use that phrase.

Shane says, *You got a problem
with your nickname?*

And then he says it again.

I nod.

Luke says, *C'mon, man,*
how about something else?

Like, Ponytail?

Shane walks
around me.

Flips my hair.

Fine. Ponytail.
Join up.

And won't mind
that I just need to use
the bathroom.

A voice calls out in response.

> *In here!*

Definitely not a custodian.

I follow the voice to
the row of sinks, where the
you hurl when we say you hurl boy
stands, body bent
over the middle sink.

> *Oh, hey,* he says.
> *Ponytail, right?*

Tae.

> *Tae. I'm Brayden.*
> *And I won the honor of*
> *handwashing the pinnies.*

He grins, revealing a mouth
full of metal.

Seriously?

> *Yup.*
> *Consider it an honor, freshman,*
> *they said.*

Guess it was stupid to
think I'd make varsity, right?

I shrug.
I'm a freshman, too.

Oh yeah?

Brayden laughs.

Whose butt did you kiss
to get out of pinny-washing duty?

PONYTAIL

Brayden says my name
like it's a consolation prize.

Like the giant blue penguin
at the summer carnival.

Aaron tried for hours to win that penguin.
Spent all his money
throwing darts at balloons.

This game is rigged, I told him.
But then I popped one
on my first try.

Aaron was so excited.

He didn't seem to care
that I won instead of him.

It was the prize
that mattered most.

I wonder if making varsity
is simply a prize to be won?

And if so, is it worth
the cost to get there?

WORD TRAVELS FAST

At dinner, Dad asks how tryouts
are going.
Mom asks about Luke.

*His mom and I keep in touch
online*, she says, before I get
the chance to ask how she knew.

> *All right,* I say,
> shoulders shrugged.

> > *Want to go for a run tonight?*
> > Dad offers.

More shoulder shrugs.

Everything hurts.
But I need to keep moving.

> *Sure.*

PEOPLE SAY

I should consider
myself lucky.

Lucky to be adopted.

Who knows what
my life would
have been like in Korea?

> Raised by a single mom
> when single moms
> are shunned by their
> families and communities.

Lucky to be in a family
with two parents
in a big house
in the suburbs.

With a brother to keep
me company
and a dad who wants
me to succeed
at everything I do.

But sometimes
that luck
feels more like
pressure.

Like I've been stuffed
into a pot and left
to boil.

Does that make me
ungrateful?

SOME UNCOMFORTABLE EVENING

Dinner.

The moms try to pretend
like we're still little kids
at the summer picnic.

They swap parenting stories
while we fake-smile
and poke at our meals.

Aaron interrupts
with facts he
learned in science class.

Something about
the reason
we pass gas.

Mom shoots her
eye arrows at him.

He
doesn't
stop
talking.
I can't help but
laugh.

Luke laughs, too.

Suddenly
we're all
burping
and laughing
and our moms are
rolling their
eyes and
trying to shush us.

Okay,
I guess this dinner
isn't so bad
after all.

UNTIL

Luke and I stand
at the kitchen sink.

I wash,
he dries.

Hey, Tae, he says.

*I really hope
you make the team, man.*

*I mean, you're so fast,
and I know Shane's impressed.*

I smile,
start to respond.

But the words
that follow are sharp—
like knives
in the soapy water.

*But can you maybe
keep quiet
about me and you?*

Being friends?

I nod.

Thanks.

It's just,
my reputation—
I'm trying to
make captain next year,
get a scholarship.

And the guys,
they don't know
that I'm adopted.

He blends in.

He's living a lie,
and I don't understand why.

But it's not my place
to judge.

BELONGING

My buddies from
the old neighborhood,
they never cared.

Never cared about
what I looked like
or where I'd come from.

I'd come from a
place they'd never been.

But that didn't matter.

All that mattered
was our friendship.

You look nice, she says.

I tug on my
new polo shirt.

*Nice will not get you
friends in high school,*
I say.

Mom sighs.

> *C'mon.*
> *I'll drive you.*

No thanks, I say.
I'll walk.

Because if I walk maybe
no one will notice
my newness,
my strangeness.

No one will notice
me.

MY FIRST DAY IS A BLUR

Guys who leave behind
a scent trail
of stale weed
and fresh cologne.

Girls who know the answers
to every question
and screech when they
see each other in the hallways.

Students who float somewhere
in between,
with styles and statements all their own.

Teachers whose laundry lists
of homework
and tests
and papers
make my head spin.

TRYOUTS: THE BAD

Shane's captain practices
were easy
compared to the drills
Coach has us do.

The returning players
fall in,
like they do these drills
in their sleep.

(They probably do.)

The rest of us struggle
to keep up.

Or maybe it's just me.

Please don't let it be
just me.

TRYOUTS: THE UGLY

The next drill—
one-on-one cutthroat.

My specialty.

Nobody has a prayer
against my speed.

But size
is another matter.

I'm up against a senior
who looks like
a mythical creature
from one of Aaron's stories.

I beat him to the ball.

He arrives
like a thundercloud.

Leans into me
as I try to shield.

Players shout
from the sideline.

NO TURN! NO TURN! (to him)

YOU GOT THIS! (to me)

I work to turn the ball
toward the net.

JUDGMENT

I feel Coach watching me.

Feel his eyes judge
every run
every mark
every ball touch.

I count players on the field.

Try to do the math.

How many of us will make the cut?

DAY ONE, DONE.

My legs ache.

My lungs scream.

I push through to the end.

The final whistle.

Bring it in, Coach shouts.

All I want to do
is collapse
onto the ground.

But we're forced to stand there,
faces to the late afternoon sun,
knees shaking.

Good work, boys, he says.

*I expect that energy
every day this week.*

Roster will be posted Monday at 3:00.

*Anyone who doesn't make the cut
is invited to try out for JV.*

If she only knew
he taught us the
crane kick
speed bag
half nelson.

I smile at the memory.

Crank out another set
of push-ups,
the songs on repeat
in my head.

HELL WEEK

Our town hits
record high temps for
September.

I don't think I've ever
sweated so much
in my entire life.

LAST SHOT TO MAKE A GOOD IMPRESSION

The whistle blows.

Our team heads off the line.

We're in control.

Heading for the goal.

Until they strip us of the ball.

I brace for the run.

Check my mark.

He's off about 10 yards.

But I've got speed.

The ball heads down the line.

I turn on my heels and race
toward my mark.

Catch the eyes of my sweeper,
who races to the ball
and gets burned by a slick move.

The forward heads straight
for the net.

I'm close,
so close.

But not close enough.

He scores.

The team celebrates.

I collapse in half,
out of breath
and full of regret.

Not the impression
I had hoped to make.

If it's not your time,
don't give up, Coach says.

There's always next year.

He sighs.
Continues his speech.

I'll post the roster online.
If your name is on it—
practice starts at 3:30.

If not, JV tryouts on the back field at 4:00.

NAME ON THE LIST

How many hours
until Monday?

WAITING

The weekend takes forever.

I try to occupy my mind
with math homework
and anime.

Mom lets me choose
the restaurant for takeout.

I pick Italian and fill up
on meatballs and greasy
garlic bread.

Someone's letting himself go,
Aaron says.

I punch his arm and tell
him to shut up.

Mom makes us stop fighting.

Tells me it'll all work out
the way it is supposed to.

Whatever that means.

SUNDAY NIGHT

My phone pings.
A number I don't recognize.

OMG I can't stand this!

I stare at the text.
Wonder who it is.

Another ping.

btw this is Brayden
aka batty

The team nicknamed him
Batty because
his ears stick straight out
like bat ears.

I add him to my contacts.

Start to respond,
then suddenly worry
that one of us will
make the team,
and the other won't.

I type *100.*

Ignore his response.

Go scoop myself a giant
bowl of chocolate ice cream.

Wonder if she has a date for Homecoming.

Gotta run, see you at practice.

      Sure, he says.

My focus shifts to Lia.

Hey, girl…

DECISION DAY

I refresh my browser 6 million
times between the 2:45 bell and 3:00.

Finally, a blue flag appears
under new messages.

My shaky finger clicks it open.
I stare, unbelieving,
at the first word:

Congratulations.

My heart sits in my throat.

I swallow it down
and read the rest of the email.

Details about practices, games, uniforms.

A text bubble appears.
A row of smiley faces and balloons.

INITIATION

I run into Brayden
on my way into the locker room.

So? he says.
He's smiling.

>   *Varsity*, I say.
>   Try to remain cool.

Same.

>   *Awesome.*

We high-five.

You, uh, you get this?
He holds up his phone.

The screen says the exact
same thing as mine.

Do you think—
He doesn't finish the thought.

We're shoved from behind.
I hold my hands out to avoid
crashing into the row of lockers.

>   *Here's two*, a voice shouts.

A chant comes in reply:

NOOBS, NOOBS, NOOBS

I drop my bag onto the ground.

Get picked up by
one of the upperclassmen
and carried across the locker room.

I look around.

There are seven of us,
some kicking and screaming,
others limp.

Brayden shouts from somewhere behind me.

Where are we going?
Guys? GUYS?

I wonder the same thing.
Then I see it.

The showers.
They're bringing us to the showers.
Fully clothed.

WAIT!
*   STOP!*

But it's too late.

WHY

Why does everyone keep
talking about my hair?

HAIR

I find out
at the end of practice.

After Coach leaves.

Before we're allowed to
call for our rides home.

Shane directs us to the side
of the building.

Two folding chairs sit,
waiting.

A small table between them.

Two electric razors.
A bottle of blue dye.

> *Westgate Warriors unite!*
> someone shouts.

The returning players step up first.

They smile and shout.

Cheer each other on
to the buzzing razor sounds.

Black strands
form a pile
around my feet.
I watch,
frozen.

WHAT HAVE I DONE?

I stare at my reflection
in the locker room mirror.

Fingers feel my prickly scalp—
raw, exposed.

I try to stay calm.

It's only hair.

It will grow back.

I'm a Westgate Warrior now.

Part of a team.

I belong.

MR. POPULARITY

The next day at school,
it's like I went viral.

Guys greet me in the halls
with *Way to go* and
Nice job, man.

Girls I don't know
smile at me.

I can't stop touching
my buzzed head.

The kid whose locker is
next to mine asks,
What's with the blue streak?

     Oh, I made varsity soccer.

Cool.

     From behind him, a girl says,
     Ponytail, right?
     My older brother's on the team.
     I hear you're really fast.

She smiles at me,
her teeth perfectly
straight and white.

*Maybe we can hang
out sometime?*

I nod.

Huh.

This whole thing
may not be
so bad after all.

PRACTICE

Coach pushes us
harder than ever.

He doesn't seem phased
by our new haircuts
or our celebrity status.

We do long field runs and sprints
until we pass out.

At least today my socks are dry.

Well, they are
before I start to sweat from the heat.

Our season runs until November.

Coach tells us to remember this feeling
when it's 45 degrees and raining.

It doesn't help.

GAME DAY

Our first game is tomorrow.

At the end of practice,
the captains call everyone
to a meeting by the sports shed.

Most of you know the drill,
Shane says.

He pulls out a large canvas bag and
tosses it on the ground.

*Noobs, you're in for a
real treat.*

Some of the guys laugh.

Brayden looks across the group
at me and raises his eyebrows
in concern.

Right.
This here is the bag of fortune.

We Warriors believe in three things:
    hard work
    tradition
    and the power of rituals.

So, before our first game,
we wear the uniforms of
all the greats
who have come before us.

He dumps the bag.

Blue and gray uniforms
land in a pile.

Shane coughs, and several boys
hold their noses.

They've never been washed, Shane says.

    Because that would be bad luck,
    a voice behind me adds.

Exactly.

Seniors get first choice.

Have at it, boys.

THE LAST SHALL BE LAST

The senior players sort through
the pile and choose the least
smelly uniforms.

By the time I step up to the pile,
the only remaining choices
reek
and are
way too big.

We have to wear these, where?
Brayden asks.

To school, Shane answers.

Tomorrow.
All day.

Underwear allowed,
but no other clothing.

And no washing.

No problem.

(GAG)

FITTING IN

Aaron laugh-snorts
when he sees me in my
"uniform."

He holds his nose with
one hand,
waves in front of his
face with the other.

Says,
*Guess this is
you
fitting in?*

AT SCHOOL

It's not easy
      to be the new kid
      to be the new Asian kid
      to be the new Asian kid wearing
      a smelly uniform
      three sizes too big.

Everyone stares.
I mean
EVERYONE.

Some laugh out loud,
some snicker behind their hands.

Some make a wide arc around me
and hold their noses.

Some reach their hands up
for a high five
and shout
WARRIORS!
as I pass by.

This school is
really strange.

BENCH WARMER

On my club team,
I'm part of the starting lineup.

I don't even wait for my club coach
to call my name,
because he always does.

From the back:
Goalie, sweeper,
defensive line.

But this is varsity.
This is the big leagues.

I haven't fully proven myself.
And so, my name isn't called.

I ride the pine.

Brayden is there, too.

We keep each other company
and cheer for our team.

I have to admit, the blue streaks
look cool.

But I'm still upset about
losing my ponytail.

I hate the way I look
in short hair.

I play for five minutes
at the end of each half.

Not much action.
We beat our opponents 4–0.

VICTORY

The good news:
Coach celebrates our win
by canceling Friday's practice.

Rest up, boys, he says.
Next week we face Seneca High.

No cakewalk there, believe me.

Groans.

Rest up, Coach repeats.
And behave yourselves this weekend.

I look over at Brayden,
but he shrugs his shoulders.

Behave ourselves.

SOON ENOUGH

Friday afternoon,
a message arrives on our player
LISTSERV:

Fri 8 p.m. Wilson Park soccer nets.
Come prepared.

I pull up a map.
Wilson Park is at the edge of town.
Residents only.

I can get there by bike.

Come prepared with what?
For what?

My stomach drops.

This must be it.

Suddenly, Coach's warning makes sense.

INITIATION

I send Luke a DM.

Is this legit?
Are they going to kidnap us?
Steal our clothes?

His response:
Don't worry, man,
I got ya.

THE WILSON PARK TRADITION

It's no big deal.
Really.

We've never gotten caught,
and everyone survives.

A little banged up, maybe,
a little sick the next day.

But it's tradition.

And like Shane says,
you don't mess with tradition.

ALL IN GOOD FUN

I made the team as a
sophomore.

Was I scared?
Nah.

I'd heard the rumors.

But I guess you don't
really know
until it happens to you.

What's there to be scared of
if it's all unknown?

The seniors took us out
to Wilson Park.

Told us not to worry—
it was all in good fun
and part of the
Westgate Warrior tradition.

So we did what they told us.

It was rough.
But I endured it.

And now it's my turn.

PARENTS

My parents never questioned
what happened that night.

Never questioned where
I'd been
or what we'd done.

Dad's told us his
frat stories from college.

So he gets it.

Mom wants me to fit in,
which is why she never pushes
the adoption thing.

Lets me keep it a secret.

FRIENDSHIP

At breakfast,
Mom asks about Tae.
Asks if we hang out.

I try not to laugh.

A junior hanging out with a freshman?

We aren't five, I say.

> *I know, but he's a good kid.*
> *Make sure you watch out for him.*

She looks at the calendar on our wall.
Then back at me.

Does she know about tonight?

LITTLE BROTHER

I guess when I think about it,
Tae is like the little brother
I never had.

At least that's how we were
when we were kids.

Chasing each other around
the playground,
nerf guns at the ready.

Splashing at the public pool,
pushing each other off the deck
until the lifeguard yelled.

At practice,
I run harder,
faster
to keep up with him
as we circle the track.

One of the guys asked
why I hang around the
"freaky Asian kid."

I lied.

Didn't tell him how racist that was.

Said something about
church camp.

Can't let them know
my secret.

But I can't
let my friend
down
either.

I text Tae:
Be cool, man.
Don't worry about tonight.
It's all in good fun.

FEAR FACTOR

Luke's text does NOT
set my mind at ease.

If anything,
it makes me more anxious.

What the heck is going to happen to us?

LIES

I tell Mom that Brayden invited me
to spend the night.

That we're going to hang
out, game, and watch movies.

She's thrilled
and doesn't question it.

Doesn't stare at me
to figure out if I'm lying.

Step One: Lie to parents.
Step Two: Don't chicken out.

THE PARK

At 8 p.m. a text arrives in the group chat.

Meet in parking lot next to port-a-potties.

No phones or smart watches.

Wear all black.

AT THE READY

I try not to think
about what comes next.

Focus on the future—
the endgame:

Acceptance.
Belonging.
Team unity.

Brayden sends a separate text:
You ready for this?

I text back the letter Y.
Put my phone on silent
and toss it into the drawer of my
nightstand.

No turning back now.

WHAT'S IN A NAME?

I leave my bike in the racks
on the far side of the park
and walk toward the
port-a-potties.

A cluster of upperclassmen
stand next to large coolers,
strange grins
on their faces.

Gather round, noobs, Shane says.
*There are seven of you
and four coolers.*

Two to each, and let's see—
he looks around the group.

His eyes land on me.

*Ponytail—ha—maybe we
we need a new nickname for you.*

Shane laughs.

I keep my hands to my sides,
afraid to feel for my hair
like a missing limb.

He walks closer.

So, Kimchi.

(more laughter)

You like to show off
your push-up skills.
You carry this cooler
on your own.

Yeah?

I look at Luke and wonder
if he'll offer to help.

He doesn't.

TEST OF STRENGTH

We carry the coolers
to the edge of the creek.
Ice crashes inside.
My arms burn from the weight.

Not here, Shane says.
He points to where
the water widens.
There.

Someone groans.

Someone says, *Shut it!*

We walk along the creek bank
and try to set the coolers down
when we arrive.

Not yet! he shouts.

My grip slips.
My back aches.

Finally, he gives the signal.
The coolers land with a thud.

All right, Shane says.
*Let's see what our new class
of Westgate Warriors
is truly made of!*

Jumping jacks.
High knees.
Squats.
Mountain climbers.

Chants in unison.

ONE
TWO
THREE
FOUR

The new players grunt
through the workout
as upperclassmen circle
through and shout in our faces.

Someone trips on a stick.
We're forced to start over.

ONE
TWO
THREE
FOUR

Finally, Shane shouts, *Enough!*

Time for the real fun!

REAL FUN?

Shane opens his backpack and
pulls out a thermos and
a stack of small plastic cups.

He sets seven cups down
on the ground in a straight line.

This, my friends,
is nectar of the gods.
Vodka courtesy of a Westgate alum.

He takes a drink from the thermos.
My brow sweats.

We line up in front of the cups.
Shane walks past us and fills them
one by one.

Facedown, plank position, he says.

Arms straight, butts down.

You fall, you drink.

Next guy falls,
you both drink.

Last guy falls,
we all drink.

Laughter.

I do the math in my head.

First guy to fall
does seven shots total.

I've never had anything
stronger than a sip of champagne
on New Year's Eve.

MIND OVER MATTER

We hold our planks
for what feels like
a lifetime.

One by one,
my teammates fall,
drink,
fall,
drink.

That's all you got?
someone shouts.

My arms shake.
My hands slip in the
slimy mud.

Breathe, Tae, breathe.

Knees, elbows, wrists,
brittle joints
scream for relief.

Finally, I fall.

There are cheers.

The cup is shoved in my face.
Its contents slide down my throat
without thought.

Everything burns.

The earth tilts
ever so slightly.

WHAT HAPPENS NEXT

The snap of something
against my back.

The sound of ice
splashing into water.

Pushed, shoved,
we fall—
no longer individuals
but a collection of bodies—
into the water.

Cold
so cold
the weight of my shoes
pulling my body
down
down
down.

I push with my arms,
reach the surface,
take a breath.

My teammates line the edge
of the lake.

They chant:
*A warrior is
strong!*

153

A warrior is
tough!

A warrior is
ready for battle!

over and over
as we tread water
and try not to sink.

I search for Brayden,
wonder how many
shots he did,
hope he's okay.

I count the heads—
one two three four five
one two three four five

I'm six.

We're supposed to be
seven.

Hey! I shout,
water working its way
into my mouth
as I struggle to stay afloat.
Hey!
Brayden!!

Chants
laughter
plastic cups clinked
in unity.

No one hears me.

BRAYDEN!
Guys! Help!

My waterlogged teammates
hear me,
start to search.

> *Over here!*

We find him
underwater.

Pull him out.

The chanting stops.

Cody, our goalie,
comes over and does CPR.

Faces in the moonlight
full of fear.
Fear of death?
Or fear of being found out?

HELP WANTED

Water drips down my face.

My brain spins from the

       shot
               cold
                       fear.

We should call 911, I say.
Get him to the hospital.

I reach for my phone.

Remember where I left it.

       No way, Cody says.

He shakes his head
in between breaths.

       Not after last time—
       after what happened to Luke.

       We promised Coach.

He presses on Brayden's chest,
counts numbers in rhythm as we

       watch
             wait
                   worry.

Finally, Brayden spits
out a mouthful of water.

Cody turns him on his side.

It's all good, guys, all good, Shane says.

Someone behind me throws up.
Their coughs echo Brayden's.

> *Let's call it a night,* Luke says.

I'm desperate to know
what happened last year.

Shane holds his arm out.

Wait.

Team.
We are a team.
Stronger together.

No one breathes a word of this.
No one.

NO EXIT

We pick up the coolers.

Walk back to the parking lot
on a trail of wet mud.

I watch my feet
one in front of the other.

Squish, squish.

My sneakers ruined.
My mouth dry.
My head pounding.

No one speaks.

IN THE PARKING LOT

Someone offers to watch Brayden
for the night.
Make sure he's okay.

Make sure he doesn't talk.

I chase after Luke.
Call his name.

He pretends like
we never met.

SECRETS

Saturday morning, I text Luke.
My unanswered bubbles
fill the screen.

I scroll through his posts,
searching for a clue.

Around a year ago, there's a bunch
of well-wishes and feel-better-soons.

A picture of Luke's feet
in slippers
and the words,
Home with the flu.

I text Luke again:
The flu?

His response comes immediately.
Meet me at the bleachers in 10.

REVEALED

Luke pulls me under the bleachers.
His hoodie is pulled tight
around his face.

Listen, he whispers.
That's old news, man.
What's done is done.

> *Luke,* I say.
> *I'm a Warrior now.*

I laugh at the irony.

> *I deserve to know.*

LUKE

SOPHOMORE YEAR

Everybody knows about
shots and shocks.

That's what they call it.

There were eight of us,
and I would have lasted longer,
but one of the seniors
had it out for me.

Our parents knew each other.
He knew I was adopted.

He whispered in my ear,

*I thought your kind
could hold their vodka.*

*Mommy and daddy
won't rescue you
this time.*
Thirty seconds into our plank,
he stepped on my back,

kicked my legs out,
made me fall
flat
on my
face.

I had to do eight shots
in less than five minutes.

Then jump
into freezing cold water.

I remember the shots.
I remember the water
like needles on my face.

And then,
I remember waking up
in the hospital.

COVER-UP

Coach came to the hospital.

He covered for me.

Told my parents there was a party
and someone spiked my drink.

I don't think they believed him.

But Coach laid on the charm,
said I was on my way
to being a top goal scorer.

With a good chance
at a D3 scholarship.

Boys make mistakes.
It's all in good fun.

That's what he said to my parents.

To the team he said,
Enough is enough.
I put my neck
on the line
for you
and it ends now.

Everyone agreed.
Guess my blackout scared them.

Guess it didn't scare them enough.

TRUTH

I tell Tae the truth
about what happened.

How our
teamwork
and
victories
are supposed to
make up for
the pain
and
humiliation.

How even if he tries
to speak out,
no one will believe him.

The team will make sure of it.

DOUBLE BIND

It looks like I have a choice.

But the reality is,
I have a choice between
two punishments.

Report the incident
and I'm a rat.
A rat that may not be believed.

Stay quiet
and nothing changes.
People continue to get hurt.

A choice between two
punishments
isn't really a choice
at all.

LITTLE BROTHER WISDOM

Mom makes a big pot
of ramen,
with separate bowls
for the additions
because she knows we all
like different things.

There's comfort in this.

But not enough
to take my mind
off Friday night.

Aaron hogs the conversation
as usual.

He tells his latest story
between loud, splashing slurps.

Something about Theseus,
the guy who defeated the Minotaur,
but in Aaron's story there are
zombies (of course)
chasing Theseus through the maze.

I tell him that's ridiculous.

He says, *Theseus will make it
as long as he doesn't
look back.*

He holds on to Ariadne's string
and focuses on defeating the monster.

I poke at the hard-boiled egg in my bowl.

The little brat
may be on to something.

FOCUS

I can't change
what's already happened:

>Luke's time in the hospital.
>Brayden nearly dead.

But I can focus on what's ahead.

THE RAT

Mom has this rule about
no cell phone
during dinner.

After we clean up,
I head for my room
to find out what I missed.

I have 45 new notifications.

What?

The team chat explodes
on my screen.

I scroll through the text bubbles
see words like
cops
suspended
rat.

My heart pounds.

Do they think it's me?

Did someone hear my conversation
with Luke?

I close the screen and call Luke.

It wasn't me, man, I swear,
he says, before I even have the chance
to speak.

      It wasn't me either, I respond.

*I know. Brayden ended up in the
hospital. Pneumonia.
Cody was with him—he made the decision.*

*Told the ER doc what happened.
Called Brayden's parents.*

Cody.

Tae, man, it's such a mess.

*They called Coach
and the cops.*

*We all have to go in
and say what happened.*

I scroll through the rest of my
notifications.

One new voicemail.
Missed call: unknown number.

Our landline rings in the distance.

      Luke, I gotta go.

PUNISHMENT

There will be an investigation.

Rumors that players will be
banned from the season.

Who will be punished?

Who
will be
punished?

WHO?

All I want to do
is play soccer.

Somehow my life
became a measure
of morality.

A question of who I want to be—
the person they expect
or a person
I respect.

HERO

When my time comes,
I don't name names.

I don't throw anyone
into the fire.

Except to say
that Cody saved
Brayden's
life.

That's interesting,
the officer responds.

She flips the pages
of her yellow legal pad.

*Cody said you were the one
who saved Brayden's life.*

Her finger follows the words
as she reads.

*Brayden must have gone under,
and Tae pulled him
to shore.*

She stares at me.
My mouth hangs open.

I'm not a hero.
I'm just a freshman.

174

He's my friend, I say.

*I was just looking out
for my friend.*

I ask her what happens next.
She says it's up to the school district.

*Players in violation of the
alcohol and hazing policies
may be kicked off the team.*

But not unless there's enough evidence.

She flips the pad to a fresh page.

*Is there anything else you
want to tell me?*

I think about Luke.

What he went through last year.
His college scholarship
on the line.

No, that's all.

CONSEQUENCES

I wish I could say
that everything worked out.

It did, I guess.
In the way one might
expect
in a town
that worships
its high school
sports team.

When privilege
comes
with a price tag.

Without proof
all they can do
is issue a warning.

Tell us we signed a contract
—no drinking
—no hazing.

We agreed to behave
sportsmanlike.
Sometimes I wonder
who defines
that term.

Who decides
what a sportsman
is like?

ON THE NEWS

When I open the
search engine on my phone,
there's a link to an article
about a kid who died
from fraternity hazing.

The family donated
his organs
and set up a foundation
in his name.

He was 19 years old.

REGRET

Mom pushes me for more
information.

She worries about the unspoken
things that hang between us
like webs.

I want to blame her
for making us move
to this fancy town
with its fancy houses
and its unwritten rules
of how to behave.

I want to remind her
that I didn't ask for any of it.

But she's crying
and trying to hug me.

So I let her.

And pretend like everything
is going to be okay.

IS IT?

Wednesday is our game
against Seneca High.

The team acts like
we haven't spent the last few days
trying not to stab each other
in the back.

Sweeping Friday under the rug
like a mess you don't want Mom
to notice.

I notice.

My body sweats
guilt
remorse
responsibility.

I run warmups with JJ and Chris,
two of the other new players.

We wear our uniforms
as badges of honor
accomplishment
survival.

We were shoved into
an ice-filled lake—

drunk
exhausted
humiliated.

Now,
we are warriors.

Silent, surviving warriors.

No one says anything.

Until JJ says, under his breath,
Wait till next year.

NEVER-ENDING CYCLE

We win the game.
But all I feel
is empty.

I text Brayden
to see how he's doing.

No response.

I text the other new guys on the team.

Look, we need to stand up for Batty.
We need to do what's right.

No response.

I try one more time.

We need to stick together.
A true Warrior
is brave
and fights for what
he believes in.

No response.

I have never felt so alone.

I BELIEVE

I believe in soccer,
and I also believe
that an athlete owes it to
his team
to be strong
fierce
and fair.

I call the detective
and tell her
everything.

FALLOUT

Local police launch
an investigation.

The school district
suspends Coach.

They say he knew what
was happening
and chose to ignore it.

Several players are also
suspended.

The varsity season
is canceled.

I worry every day
about retaliation.

That they will come
after me
for being a rat.

The detective assures me
she'll keep my name
out of it.

She also says other players
came forward.

I'll never know if that was
the truth.

Brayden's family files a lawsuit
against the district
and switches him to a private school.

I keep my head down,
play club soccer in the spring,
and wait for another
chance to earn
my varsity letter.

SEPTEMBER

The team is different this year.

No shaved heads,
blue streak optional.

I'm growing my hair
long again, and I left it
plain black.

We still wore the old uniforms,
but somebody's dad
offered to wash them.

Our new coach is tough—he
yells when we drag on sprints
or miss the ball—
but he sat us down on the first day
and talked about what it truly
means to be
sportsmanlike.

He paces the sidelines now
as we listen for the whistle.

Our first game against Seneca High.

I'm starting at left D,
Luke is up at striker.

There's a college recruiter
in the stands.

Seneca has the kickoff,
and they come after us
in a blaze of cleats.

Past the center mid,
long ball to the right wing.

I anticipate,
stop the pass before it reaches him.

Look up.
Green turf ahead.

Dribble, dribble, think.

A midfielder runs toward me.
I look for an open pass,
do a give and go with JJ,
head up the line.

There is cheering,
the sound of my name,
but I barely hear it.

I'm focused on the ball at my feet,
the muscles in my legs as they
tear up the ground in front of me.

I look, see Luke race toward the net,
hands out in front,
waiting for the pass.

Tae!
I use my left foot to drill the ball
across the field.

Just enough lift to sail past
the line of defenders.

Luke runs to meet the pass
connects with his head
sends the ball straight into
the net.

Yeah, man! he shouts.

My heart pounds as we run toward
midfield, shouts and high fives
all around.

The game is an intense back-and-forth
that ends in victory.

Back at the bench,
everyone checks their phones.

I reach for mine.
Open the text:

Celebration tonight
8 p.m.
Wilson Park.

I search the faces around me.
All I know is—this time,
things will be different
on my watch.

WANT TO KEEP READING?

If you liked this book, check out another
book from West 44 Books:

MANNING UP
BY BEE WALSH

ISBN: 9781538382677

COACH SAYS

Coach says

I need to keep
my head down
when I rush
the defensive end.

Running back.
Head down.
Eyes up.
Take him
down.

Coach says

I need to lift
my feet.

Coach says

I need to focus.

Coach says

I have to be
ready for Friday.

I have to be
ready.

EYES ON THE PRIZE

Today at practice,
Coach asks me
where I see myself
in five years.

Five years.

> "Here, I guess."

> "No son,
> where do you want
> to be?"

> "Here, I guess."

> "Jack,
> you need to get
> your eyes on the prize."

The prize.

What is
the prize?

ANYTHING

I'd give anything
to be able
to put on
invisible clothes
like that wizard kid
in that book.

Walk around
and no one
would look
at me.

No one
would pat me
on the shoulder

and ask me
about the game.

No one
would ask me
how my mother

is holding up.

I could do
anything
and no one
would say anything
about it.

MOM

Mom had me
when she was
my age
now.

Seventeen.

She had Beth
two years later.

She said
from the moment
she met
our dad
when she was 12

in the same town
we live in now

that she was
gonna love him
for the rest
of her life.

When Dad died
eight years after
I was born,

I heard Mom cry
and make sounds
I didn't know
people could make.

Beth and I don't
talk about it
but I hope
every day
that she doesn't
remember.

But it never
stopped Mom
from putting
dinner on the table.
Or putting
herself through
night school
to become
a paralegal.

These days,
she helps people
who are here illegally
figure out
their rights
and how
they're gonna
feed their kids,
too.

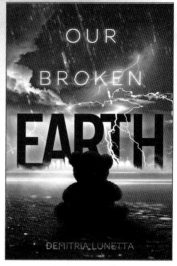

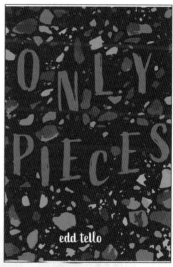

ABOUT THE AUTHOR

Sandi Van is a writer, counselor, and former soccer coach from Buffalo, New York. She is the author of young adult verse novels, *Second in Command, Listen Up*, and *Everything It Takes*. Mom to two boys, both adopted from South Korea, Sandi hates the term soccer mom but embraces her role as one and loves cheering from the sidelines. You can follow her on social media @sandivanwrites or visit her website at Sandivan.com.